RECEIVED
JUN   2019
BY

NO LONGER PROPERTY OF
SEATTLE PUBLIC LIBRARY

Galia Bernstein

Leyla

Abrams Books for Young Readers

New York

Leyla has a mother and a father.

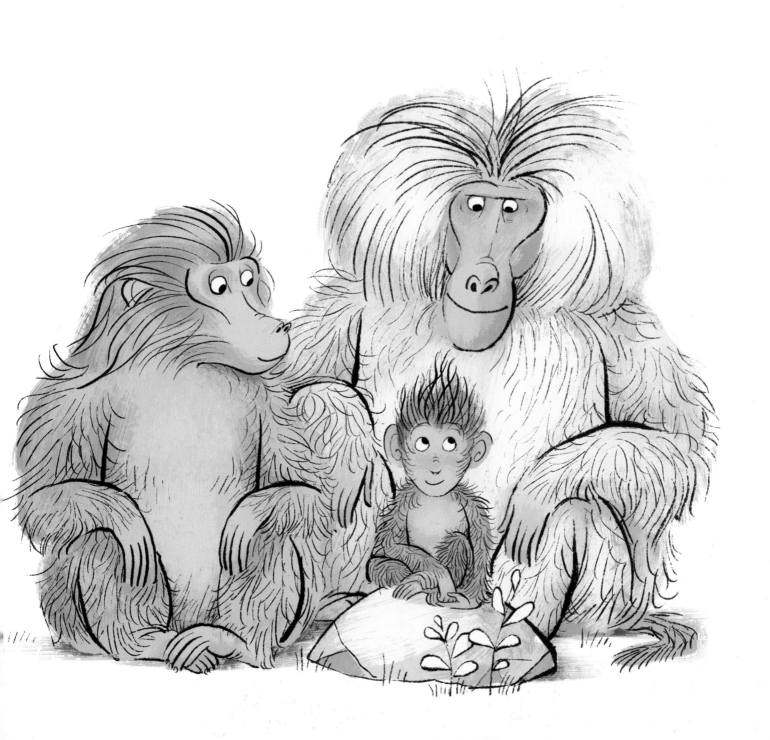

And nine aunts and twenty-three cousins.

That's too many!

They always want to hug and kiss her. Yuck!

They always want to groom her.

She's not even dirty!

They are always busy,

always fussy,

always noisy.

She's *trying* to take a nap!

So Leyla ran away.

She ran until she couldn't see them anymore.

She ran and ran until she couldn't smell them anymore.

She ran and ran and ran until she couldn't hear them anymore.

It was so quiet . . .

Nothing around but Leyla.

And some sharp rocks.

And a lizard.

EEEEEEEEEP!!!

"I'm Leyla, what's your name?"

The lizard didn't answer.

"I hurt my foot. Do you want to kiss it better?"

The lizard opened one eye. "*Shhh*," he said. "I'm busy."

"You're not doing anything," said Leyla.

"I'm very busy doing nothing."

"How do you do nothing?"

"Well . . ." said the lizard.

"To do nothing, you sit perfectly still, feel the sun on your skin, listen to the leaves rustling in the wind and the insects buzzing in the air, and think of nothing at all.

Now, close your eyes . . ."

When Leyla opened her eyes, the lizard was in the
same spot, but the sun was on the other side of the sky.
She suddenly missed her family.
It was time to go home.

"Can I come back and do nothing with you again?" she asked.

"You can," said the lizard as he closed his eyes.

"I'm always around."

Leyla turned around and ran.

She ran until she could hear them again.

She ran and ran until she could smell them again.

She ran and ran and ran until she could see them again.

There they were: her family!

She told them about her adventure.

"I ran and ran!"

"It was so hot!"

"The grass was *this* tall!"

She told them she met a lizard.

"He was *this* big!"

They thought she was very brave and wanted to know if she was all right.

Then she remembered.

"I hurt my foot.

Do you want to kiss it better?"

They *ALL* wanted to kiss it better!

That night, in her mother's arms, Leyla didn't mind the noise.
She remembered the sun and the breeze, the leaves and the insects,
and the lizard's voice telling her to close her eyes and think of
nothing at all.

But from then on, whenever it all got a bit too much,

she went to see the lizard.

And the lizard was always there.

For Maya and Alon
—G.B.

The art for this book was created digitally with applied hand-painted textures.

Cataloging-in-Publication Data has been applied for and may be obtained from the Library of Congress.

ISBN 978-1-4197-3543-1

Copyright © 2019 Galia Bernstein
Book design by Pamela Notarantonio

Published in 2019 by Abrams Books for Young Readers, an imprint of ABRAMS. All rights reserved. No portion of this book may be reproduced, stored in a retrieval system, or transmitted in any form or by any means, mechanical, electronic, photocopying, recording, or otherwise, without written permission from the publisher.

Printed and bound in China
10 9 8 7 6 5 4 3 2 1

Abrams Books for Young Readers are available at special discounts when purchased in quantity for premiums and promotions as well as fundraising or educational use. Special editions can also be created to specification. For details, contact specialsales@abramsbooks.com or the address below.

Abrams® is a registered trademark of Harry N. Abrams, Inc.

ABRAMS The Art of Books
195 Broadway, New York, NY 10007
abramsbooks.com

Author's Note

Hamadryas baboons, like Leyla, live in loud, large, and loving families, called troops, along the southern shores of the Red Sea. This semidesert environment includes Ethiopia, Somalia, and parts of the Arabian Peninsula. The baboon troops are always together—they travel together, sleep together, and raise their babies together.

I came up with the idea for this book while watching the small troop of hamadryas baboons that lives at the Prospect Park Zoo in Brooklyn. A baby boy was taking his first steps and, much like a human baby, became the center of attention. It made me think about different people in my life and how they would react to so much family in close quarters.

And that's how *Leyla* came to be. I was inspired by the idea of a little baboon who might find this kind of life a bit overwhelming—a clever and opinionated young girl who was ready to carve her own path and discover the value of spending time away from it all. I hope you will love her as much as I do, but not with too many hugs and kisses . . . *Yuck*.